See What I Can Play!

Published in 2010 by Windmill Books, LLC
303 Park Avenue South, Suite # 1280, New York, NY 10010-3657

Adaptations to North American Edition © 2010 Windmill Books

© 2007 Autumn Publishing
Published in 2007 by Autumn Publishing
A division of Bonnier Media Ltd.,
Chichester, West Sussex, UK PO20 7EQ.

CREDITS:
Illustrator: Pauline Siewert

                          Publisher Cataloging Data
Siewert, Pauline
          See what I can play! – North American ed. / illustrated by Pauline Siewert.
                    p. cm. – (Watch this!)
          Summary: While playing, little girls imagine being a fairy, a dog walker,
a bride, a horseback rider, and more.
          ISBN 978-1-60754-461-6 (hardback) – ISBN 978-1-60754-462-3 (pbk.)
ISBN 978-1-60754-460-9 (6-pack)
          1. Play—Juvenile fiction   2. Imagination—Juvenile fiction
[1. Play—Fiction   2. Imagination—Fiction]   I. Title   II. Series
          [E]—dc22

Manufactured in the United States of America.

See What I Can Play!

Illustrated by Pauline Siewert

alphabet
soup™
an imprint of
WINDMILL BOOKS™
New York

I can play with my wand and...

...I'm a fairy!

I can play in the snow and...

...I'm a mountain climber!

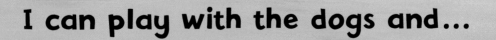

I can play with the dogs and...

...I'm a dog walker!

I can play with my camera and...

...I'm a photographer!

I can play with the daisies and...

...I'm a bride!

I can play on the horse and...

...I'm a horseback rider!

I can keep my eye on the ball, and...

...I'm a tennis champion!

For more great fiction and nonfiction, go to windmillbooks.com.